MOONWALKER

The Storybook

Michael Jackson is known all over the world. His music can be heard everywhere from Africa to Thailand to France to Australia. The *Guinness Book of World Records* lists his album *Thriller* as the biggest-selling album of all time—*ever!*—with over 40 million copies sold. He has performed for Presidents and Kings and millions of people. He has performed the songs from his record-breaking album *Bad* to sold-out concert audiences the world over. In fact, *Bad* is the first album in history to have *five* #1 singles. During the 1980s, Michael has achieved *nine* #1 hits on the *Billboard* Hot 100—more than any other artist in this decade. He was given an award by the President of the United States for his many amazing achievements.

MOONWALKER

The Storybook

Original story by
Michael Jackson

Illustrated with scenes from
the screenplay by David Newman

HEINEMANN : LONDON

William Heinemann Ltd
Michelin House, 81 Fulham Road, London SW3 6RB

LONDON MELBOURNE AUCKLAND

First published in Great Britain 1988

British Library Cataloguing in Publication Data

Jackson, Michael, *1958–*
Moonwalker
1. Pop music. Jackson, Michael, 1958–
Illustrations
I. Title
784.5'0092'4

ISBN 0 434 37043 6

Printed and bound in Great Britain by
Richard Clay Ltd, Norwich, Norfolk

When he was five years old he was a member of the Jackson 5, so he's been singing and dancing for most of his life. Audiences around the world have been astounded by his extraordinary talent. The man who made the Moonwalk more famous than NASA is. . .

Michael Jackson. Michael always had a dream. He cannot remember a time when it wasn't there. He would think about the dream as he made wishes on stars or blew out candles. He also worked hard to help this dream along. He wanted to sing and dance all over the world and touch the lives of people everywhere. He loves sharing his talents with everyone and he believes we all have something to share.

Michael's songs have special meanings and messages. They ask people to stop and think about their actions, think about other people, think about the world.

Michael likes to remind the millions of people everywhere that a single person *can* make a difference, *can* change the world and make it a better place. In the song "Man in the Mirror," he tells people to help change the world by changing themselves first. One small change in your own life can, as if by magic, create a chain reaction that helps others, who, in turn, help more people until everyone everywhere has been touched and changed. Suddenly the world *is* a better place. Come follow Michael and his friends as they attempt to change the world they've discovered.

On a beautiful spring day Michael and his pal Katy
are sitting in a meadow, enjoying the warmth of the sun
with Katy's dog Skipper.

Their friends Sean and Zeke see them and run over to join them. They have a soccer ball and soon the four friends are running all over the meadow as Skipper watches, eager to join the game.

Soon, watching all the fun is too much for Skipper and he joins the game uninvited. He gets a little carried away, however, and, in his excitement, races into the woods with the soccer ball clamped in his mouth. The friends run after him and that makes the game Skipper has just invented all the more fun. He runs faster and soon disappears from sight.

Once they get deep into the woods, Michael and Katy are separated from Sean and Zeke. They call Skipper's name and look everywhere, but their shouts go unanswered. When they stumble across the entrance to a cave, they know they have to take a look inside because it would be just like Skipper to run in there to hide. The cave is deserted and filled with cobwebs, but it intrigues them.

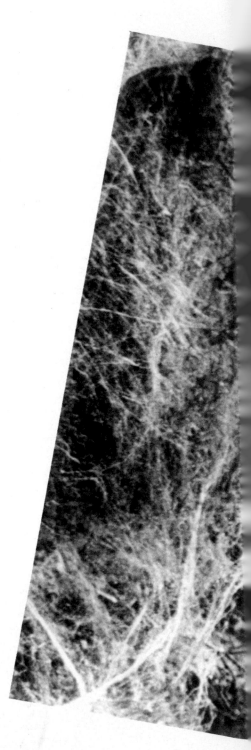

On one of the walls is a strange carving that resembles a spider.

Michael is fascinated by the odd spiderlike carving and places his hand over it. Suddenly it begins to glow and a wall of the cave begins to move. Katy is scared and wants to leave, but the wall has shifted to reveal a secret doorway. Michael convinces Katy that they should see what lies ahead.

Michael and Katy move quietly through a long passageway and find themselves staring down at a huge laboratory that's bustling with activity.

They carefully conceal their presence as they listen to the voice of an evil man named Mr. Big, who is telling his troops of a plan he has to turn children everywhere into helpless drug addicts.

Mr. Big sees Michael and Katy and realizes that his plans have been overheard. He must get them before they try to stop his evil plan. Michael and Katy run from the cave as quickly as they can.

Safely back in the city, Michael sends Katy to find Zeke and Sean while he tries to figure out how to deal with Mr. Big and his terrible troopers. Michael tells Katy to get the boys and meet him later at Club 30s.

Michael, knowing he must find a way to foil Mr. Big's plans, is deep in thought, staring at the beautiful night sky for inspiration, when suddenly he senses danger. Mr. Big and his soldiers are nearby and they see Michael standing on the steps of his apartment building.

In a split second, the quiet of the night is shattered by machine-gun fire. Bullets are flying everywhere, roaring past Michael as they break windows and damage buildings. Smoke has now filled the eerie night when all of a sudden everything becomes deadly silent.

Because of the smoke, Mr. Big and his troopers are unable to see Michael, but Mr. Big is sure they will find him sprawled on the ground. Mr. Big walks quietly out from behind his men and finds that Michael has disappeared!

Mr. Big cannot believe his eyes. He turns to his troopers and shouts instructions. Suddenly they see Michael running down the street and around a corner, out of sight. Mr. Big sends his men in pursuit. They must get Michael. *Now!*

Michael has taken a wrong turn and finds himself in a dead-end alley with no possible way out. He can hear the loud pursuing footsteps of Mr. Big and his heavily armed men.

Michael looks up at the beautiful night sky, as if he is looking for an answer in the stars. Perhaps he is—and perhaps there *is* magic in that sky.

Mr. Big assembles his troops at the opening of the alley and has each man aim his gun down the shadowy dead-end passage. The soldiers are ready to open fire when—suddenly—a large and very shiny silver car roars out of the alley. Mr. Big can tell that this vehicle is much more than a car and he wants it as badly as he wants Michael.

Mr. Big orders his men to open fire! A dizzying number of shots are fired at the beautiful car, but the bullets just bounce off. Above the roar of the guns, the car's enormous engine gives off its own very loud noises as the engine revs and the car begins to race toward the evil men. They all watch with amazement as the car sails into the air and over their heads, trailing a tail of fire behind it. Michael has escaped once again.

Mr. Big watches as the car speeds up the street and out of sight, going much too quickly for anyone to follow it.

The car rolls to a stop around the corner from Club 30s, where Michael promised to meet his friends.

Meanwhile Sean and Zeke have found Skipper back in
the meadow, playfully awaiting Michael and the kids.
Unable to find Michael and Katy, the boys finally leave.
Later it is Katy who finds them. She asks them to go with
her to Club 30s to wait for Michael and they
enthusiastically agree. When they get to the club, no one
is there. As a matter of fact, it looks as if there hasn't been
anyone in or around the club for a very long time.

The dusty old place is creepy and dirty, so the kids decide to wait outside in a little alley and keep an eye out for Michael.

Michael doesn't know the kids are waiting for him nearby, so he enters the club, thinking they're inside. A bright blinding light flashes as Michael enters. When he opens his eyes again, the light has faded and the club has been transformed into a hot night spot right out of the 1930s. Michael's clothes have changed too. He's now wearing a cool suit and a big white hat.

Michael sees a jukebox across the room, digs deeply into a pocket and finds a shiny coin that he flips through the air. As if by magic, the coin drops neatly into the slot, the jukebox lights up and wonderful music begins to play.

Suddenly the club is filled with people and everyone begins to dance with Michael as he sings "Smooth Criminal."

As he came into the window,
It was the sound of a crescendo.

Annie, are you okay?
So, Annie, are you okay?
Are you okay, Annie?

Okay, I want everybody to clear the area right now!
Aaow!

So they went into the outway.
It was Sunday, what a black day.

Annie, are you okay?
So, Annie, are you okay?

Are you okay, Annie?
You've been hit by . . .
You've been hit by a
smooth criminal.

Katy, Sean and Zeke haven't seen Michael arrive as they wait out in the alley. They're sure that he wouldn't linger inside the dusty old club any more than they would. But suddenly Katy hears music coming from inside the club. She looks in through one of the windows and smiles when she sees Michael. Not only is he safe, but he is having a wonderful time. She calls to Zeke and Sean, who rush over to watch Michael and the dancers as they stride around the floor.

Zeke jumps to the ground and begins to dance like Michael. "I taught Michael everything he knows about dancing," Zeke insists as he continues to dance below the window.

Mr. Big and his men have followed Michael to Club 30s, refusing to give up. They surround the building and open fire, shooting into the club. When the noise from their guns finally stops and the smoke clears, Michael is standing unhurt, surveying what's left of the damaged club.

When the children saw Mr. Big arrive, they were startled and tried to run away, but Mr. Big caught Katy. He has taken her prisoner to lure Michael into a trap because Mr. Big knows that wherever Katy goes, Michael will follow.

When Michael learns that Mr. Big has taken Katy
away with him, he's desperate to find her. He knows
she's in terrible danger.

Unsure that he'll be able to find her quickly enough,
Michael decides to allow himself to be captured by
several of Mr. Big's men.

Michael is taken back to the woods where he and Katy searched for Skipper. At the entrance to Mr. Big's laboratory, dozens of troopers stand guard on the high walls surrounding the place.

Michael is completely surrounded and there seems to be no escape.

The great entrance to the laboratory slides open with a rumble. Standing in the white light is Mr. Big, holding tightly to a very scared little Katy. When she sees Michael, she screams his name and tries to run to him.

After fleeing from the club, Zeke and Sean were looking for Michael when they saw the soldiers taking him away. They followed quietly and crept to the top of a nearby hill to see what was going on down below. They look at all the soldiers, knowing there is nothing they can do to help their friends.

Katy struggles with Mr. Big, causing the evil man to take his eyes off of Michael, who then lunges forward to try and free Katy. As Mr. Big defends himself from Michael and yells for his troops, Katy slips from his grasp.

In the awful confusion that follows, Katy manages to escape. She scrambles up the nearby hill and into Sean and Zeke's joyous embrace. The three friends are happy to be together again, but they are very worried about Michael, who is still in big trouble down below.

Michael, who often finds magical strength from the stars in the night sky, looks up into the twinkling velvet sky as if he's searching for a way to fight off the evil army he's facing. Suddenly Michael is aware of Mr. Big's disappearance. He looks all around him as a rock slides away from a large hole in the side of Mr. Big's mountain to reveal a gigantic laser gun with Mr. Big at the trigger.

The troopers notice something strange happening to Michael. His skin begins to change to a smooth silvery color and he begins to take on the shape of a robot—a magnificent robot—capable of destroying Mr. Big's army.

Seeing that his men will be easily defeated by Michael, Mr. Big prepares for a final deadly battle.

Michael continues to change shape.
Before everyone's astonished eyes he becomes
a spaceship that rises steadily from the ground, ready to do
battle with the terrible Mr. Big and end his evil plot against the
children of the world.

Mr. Big switches his lasers to full power, takes aim and fires, certain that Michael will not have the strength to fight back.

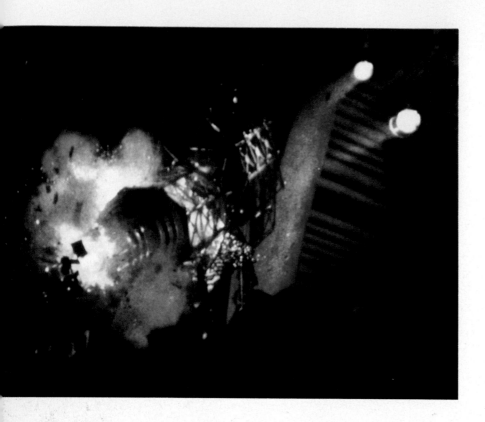

The force field surrounding the mighty
spaceship protects Michael and acts as
a reflector. Mr. Big's laser beams bounce off
the spaceship and return, hurtling toward
the gun and Mr. Big. A huge explosion
marks the end of a wicked man and his
wicked scheme.

The spaceship rises triumphantly above the ruins of the laboratory and flies over to where Katy, Sean and Zeke are waiting.

Katy, Zeke and Sean are filled with joy. Michael has saved them and all of the children of the world. It is a great day for everyone.

Michael tells his friends that he must leave. He has accomplished a great deal here, but he cannot stay any longer. They say a sad goodbye to their dear friend.

The kids miss Michael from the moment he leaves. The next day they meet outside of Club 30s, where they sit and talk about how quickly their lives have been changed, how one man really can make a difference, just like Michael told them. They're all very sad, but Katy never gives up hope that Michael will return to them . . . somehow.

Far down the street Katy sees an oddly familiar-looking man. There's something about the way he walks, almost as if his feet don't touch the ground. Suddenly all three of them know that their wish has come true. Michael has returned!

Together the four friends enter Club 30s and are caught in the blinding white light. When the light fades and they open their eyes, Katy, Zeke and Sean are backstage at a Michael Jackson concert. Michael is performing before a huge audience and singing "Come Together."

The end.